British Library Cataloguing in Publication Data
A catalogue record for this book is available from the British Library
ISBN 0340 62011 0 Hardback
ISBN 0340 65672 7 Paperback

Text copyright © Vivian French 1996
Illustrations copyright © Alison Bartlett 1996
The rights of Vivian French to be identified as the Author of the Work
and the rights of Alison Bartlett to be identified as the Illustrator of the Work
have been asserted by them in accordance with the
Copyright, Design and Patents Act 1988
10 9 8 7 6 5 4 3 2
First published 1996
by Hodder Children's Books,
a division of Hodder Headline plc,
338 Euston Road, London NW1 3BH
Printed in Singapore
All rights reserved

Bob the Dog

Vivian French
and
Alison Bartlett

Hodder
Children's
Books

a division of Hodder Headline plc

The sun was shining and the birds were singing.
Bob the dog woke up, stretched and hurried off
to have his breakfast.
But his bowl was empty.

Green Bird was sitting and squawking happily
in the tree.

Bob explained that he hadn't had any breakfast.
"Someone must have eaten it," said Green Bird.
"There were biscuits in your bowl. And gravy."

Bob howled. "Yowl!
My favourite!" He was hungry.
He decided to find out who had taken
his biscuits and gravy. He was going to
teach them a lesson.
"Grrr! I'll catch that thief," he growled.

Smitty Small Dog was burying a bone.
"You *do* look fierce," he said.

"Woof!" said Bob and told Smitty about his
disappearing breakfast and his empty bowl.

Smitty said he didn't know anything about it.
He was too busy with his bone to bother
with anyone else's breakfast.
"Grrr! I'll catch that thief and biff him!"
growled Bob.

Olly Old Dog was snoozing in the sunshine.
"Woof woof!" said Bob. "Did *you* eat
my breakfast?"

Olly Old Dog sighed. He said he was too old to eat other people's breakfasts.
"Grr! I'll catch that thief and biff him and bop him!" growled Bob and on he stamped.

Bob screeched to a stop. There was Smiler Cat
cleaning her whiskers. A big bowl of kitty
crunchies lay untouched beside her.
"Did *you* eat my breakfast?" Bob asked.

Smiler said no.
She said she didn't like biscuits and gravy.
She said she didn't like dogs.
And she wanted Bob to GO AWAY.

Bob went stamping on.

Green Bird flapped down beside him.

"Who ate my breakfast?" said Bob miserably.

"It wasn't Smitty or Olly or Smiler. Smitty has a bone, Olly's too old and Smiler doesn't like biscuits and gravy."

Green Bird looked thoughtful.
"Your bowl was empty," she said.
"*How* did Smiler know your breakfast
was biscuits and gravy?
Did you tell her?"
Bob shook his head.
"So how did she know?" Green Bird
squawked excitedly.

"G'RRR!" Bob rushed off.
Smiler heard him coming and jumped
onto the fence.
"YOU ATE MY BREAKFAST!" Bob shouted.

Smiler smiled. "Meeow," she said. "It was
very tasty," and she licked her lips.
"I'm going to chase you and catch you
and biff you and bop you!" yelled Bob.

Bob

"Catch me if you can," said Smiler and she tiptoed along the top of the fence.

Bob sat down. He scratched his ears, and he thought.

"WOOF!" said Bob, and dashed up
Smiler's path. Her bowl of kitty crunchies
was still there. Smiler watched from the fence
as Bob ate every single one.

"Sssst!" hissed Smiler.
But Bob was pleased.
At last he'd had his breakfast.
"Woof," he grinned. "*That* was very tasty!"